*With love to my wonderful Theo, who would only sit still to look
at the pictures, but now even manages to wait for his pudding!*

OXFORD
UNIVERSITY PRESS

Great Clarendon Street, Oxford OX2 6DP

Oxford University Press is a department of the University of Oxford.
It furthers the University's objective of excellence in research, scholarship,
and education by publishing worldwide in

Oxford   New York

Auckland   Cape Town   Dar es Salaam   Hong Kong   Karachi
Kuala Lumpur   Madrid   Melbourne   Mexico City   Nairobi
New Delhi   Shanghai   Taipei   Toronto

With offices in

Argentina   Austria   Brazil   Chile   Czech Republic   France   Greece
Guatemala   Hungary   Italy   Japan   Poland   Portugal   Singapore
South Korea   Switzerland   Thailand   Turkey   Ukraine   Vietnam

Oxford is a registered trade mark of Oxford University Press
in the UK and in certain other countries

British Library Cataloguing in Publication Data available

ISBN: 978-0-19-272081-8 (hardback)
ISBN: 978-0-19-272080-1 (paperback)

3 5 7 9 10 8 6 4 2

Printed in China

Hurry Up and Slow Down

LAYN MARLOW

OXFORD
UNIVERSITY PRESS

Hare is nearly always in a hurry.

Tortoise, however, is not.

Tortoise likes to sleep late in the mornings.

'Hurry up and wake up!'

And do some stretching
before he leaves his bed.

'Hurry up
and Get up!'

Tortoise is cautious when crossing the stream.

'Hurry up
and keep up!'

He likes to take his time over lunch.
'Hurry up and eat up!'

And chew each leaf at least eleventy times.
'Is it time for pudding?'

When Tortoise plays
a game, he plays slowly
and thoughtfully.

He doesn't mess about,
and is always careful to
put things away just so.

'Hurry up
and tidy up!'

Tortoise *doesn't* like having
to tidy all over again.

'Oops!'

But when it is time for Hare to bounce
into bed, what Tortoise likes most of all
is to sip a cup of chamomile tea in peace.

Hare, however,
has other ideas.

'Can we
have a
story?'

'Just one?'

'Oh please,
please,
pleeeease?'

'You're SO
good at reading,
Tortoise.'

So Tortoise opens their favourite picture book and begins to read the words out loud.

In no time at all,
he reads all the words
on the first page.

The second page . . .

and the third are
over in a flash.

The fourth flies by in the wink of an
eye and Tortoise goes on to the fifth.

He is just about to turn the page again,
when Hare cries . . .

'We need to take our time, Tortoise.
We need to look at the pictures!'

Tortoise looks longingly at his cup of
chamomile tea which is going cold.

Then he looks at Hare and smiles and says . . .

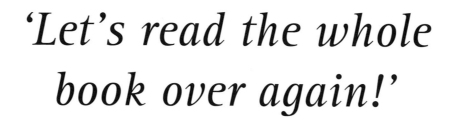

'Let's read the whole
book over again!'